Best Friends

Written by Michèle Dufresne · Illustrated by Max Stasiuk

PIONEER VALLEY EDUCATIONAL PRESS, INC.

This is Clarence.

Clarence is a dragon.

This is Lily.

Lily is a fairy.

Lily and Clarence are best friends.

"Come on," said Clarence.

"Let's go flying."

Lily got onto Clarence's back.

"Yes! Let's go," she said.

They went up, up, up.

"Oh, no," said Lily.

"Oh, no!"

"Where is Lily?" said Clarence.

"Where did she go?"

Clarence went to look for Lily.

11

"Help!" called Lily.

"Help! Help!"

"Lily is calling for help!"
said Clarence. "Where is she?"

"I'm coming," he called.

"Where are you?"

"Look up," said Lily.

"I'm up in the tree,

and I can't get down!"

"Why are you up in this tree?" said Clarence.